THE GRAPHIC
SHAKESPEARE SERIES

ROMEO & JULIET

Published by
Evans Brothers Limited
2A Portman Mansions
Chiltern Street
London W1M 1LE

© in the modern text Hilary Burningham 1997
© in the illustrations Evans Brothers Ltd 1997
Designed by Design Systems Ltd.

British Library Cataloguing in Publication Data.
Burningham, Hilary
  Romeo and Juliet. – (The graphic Shakespeare series)
  1. Children's plays, English
  I. Title II. Fripp, Emily III. Shakespeare, William 1564-1616
  822.3'3

ISBN 0 237 517841

Printed in Hong Kong by Wing King Tong Co Ltd

THE GRAPHIC SHAKESPEARE SERIES

ROMEO & JULIET

RETOLD BY HILARY BURNINGHAM
ILLUSTRATED BY EMILY FRIPP

EVANS BROTHERS LIMITED

THE CHARACTERS IN THE PLAY

Romeo — son of Montague

Juliet — daughter of Capulet

Benvolio — nephew of Montague and friend of Romeo and Mercutio

Tybalt — nephew of Lady Capulet

Old Capulet — head of a family of Verona

Lady Capulet — wife of Old Capulet

Old Montague — head of a family of Verona

Lady Montague — wife of Old Montague

Paris — a young count

Nurse — Juliet's nurse

Mercutio — friend of Romeo

Prince Escalus — Prince of Verona

Friar Laurence — priest

Apothecary — chemist

PORTRAIT GALLERY

Romeo

Juliet

Benvolio

Tybalt

Old Capulet

Lady Capulet

Old Montague

Lady Montague

Paris

Nurse

Mercutio

Prince Escalus

Friar Laurence

Apothecary

ACT 1

Many years ago, there were two families, the Montagues and the Capulets. They lived in a town called Verona in Italy. Both families were very rich.

The Montagues hated the Capulets and the Capulets hated the Montagues. No one could really remember the reason. Even their servants would fight each other when they met on the street.

One day, two Capulet servants, Gregory and Sampson, met two Montague servants. They started a fight.

Soon, other people joined in. Benvolio, a Montague, didn't like the fighting. He tried to stop it. Tybalt, a Capulet, picked a fight with Benvolio.

Tybalt hated all the Montagues. He even hated the idea of peace. Tybalt was always looking for trouble.

Old Capulet and old Montague, the heads of the two families, wanted to join in the fighting. Lady Capulet and Lady Montague tried to stop them.

SAMPSON: Draw, if you be men. Gregory, remember thy slashing blow.

Prince Escalus, the ruler of Verona, was very angry. The fighting between the Montagues and the Capulets had gone on long enough. The streets weren't safe. All the people had started to carry weapons.

He said that the next person to start a fight would be punished. The punishment would be death.

He told the people to go home.

PRINCE: If ever you disturb our streets again,
         Your lives shall pay the forfeit of the peace.

Old Montague and Lady Montague asked Benvolio about the trouble. Benvolio said that he had tried to stop the fight. Tybalt came along and picked a fight. Tybalt was a troublemaker.

The Montagues were worried about their son, Romeo. He was always sad and didn't want to speak to anyone. Benvolio, Romeo's cousin, was also his close friend. He would talk to Romeo. Maybe he could find out why Romeo was so unhappy.

BENVOLIO: See, where he comes. So please you step aside.
I'll know his grievance or be much denied.

Benvolio was a very understanding person. Benvolio had a chat with Romeo. Romeo was in love, but refused to tell Benvolio the name of the lady he loved. The lady he loved had vowed[1] never to love any man. No wonder Romeo was sad. He knew he had no chance with this lady, yet still he loved her.

Benvolio hated to see Romeo so unhappy. He said that Romeo should get to know other young ladies. Romeo was sure that he could never love anyone else.

[1]vowed – made a solemn promise before God.

BENVOLIO: Be ruled by me – forget to think of her.
ROMEO: O, teach me how I should forget to think!
BENVOLIO: By giving liberty unto thine eyes.
Examine other beauties.

Lord and Lady Capulet had a daughter named Juliet. The County[1] Paris wanted to marry her. Lord Capulet told him that Juliet was only fourteen years old. She was too young to be married. Paris could get to know Juliet. She might learn to love him after a while.

The Capulets were giving a party that night. Paris could see Juliet. Perhaps she would like him!

Old Capulet gave a list of the guests to a servant. He was supposed to go and invite all the people on the list. Old Capulet didn't know that the servant couldn't read!

[1]County – a title, like Lord or Sir.

CAPULET: Go, sirrah, trudge about
Through fair Verona; find those persons out
Whose names are written there, and to them say,
My house and welcome on their pleasure stay.

Old Capulet gave his list of guests to a servant who couldn't read! The servant had to find someone to read the list for him.

At that moment, along came Romeo and Benvolio. The servant asked them to help him with the list.

Romeo read the list aloud. The lady he loved was called Rosaline. Her name was on the list.

The servant invited Romeo and Benvolio to the party. He didn't know they were Montagues.

Benvolio had a good idea. He said they should go to the Capulets' party. There would be lots of pretty girls there. Romeo might see that there were other girls he could love.

Romeo said he would go, but he was sure he would never change his mind about Rosaline.

BENVOLIO: At this same ancient feast of Capulet's
Sups the fair Rosaline whom thou so loves,
With all the admired beauties of Verona.
Go thither, and with untainted eye
Compare her face with some that I shall show,
And I will make thee think thy swan a crow.

At the Capulets' house, Lady Capulet wanted to talk to Juliet.

Juliet was with her nurse. The nurse had been with her since she was a little girl. The nurse chattered on and on. Lady Capulet and Juliet both had to tell her to be quiet.

Lady Capulet asked Juliet if she would like to get married. Juliet was fourteen years old. She hadn't thought about marriage.

The County Paris wanted to marry her. He was coming to the party that night.

Juliet said she would meet him and get to know him. That was what her parents wanted her to do. Juliet wanted to please her parents.

LADY CAPULET: Speak briefly, can you like of Paris' love?
JULIET: I'll look to like, if looking liking move.
But no more deep will I endart mine eye
Than your consent gives strength to make
it fly.

Romeo, Benvolio, Mercutio (another friend of Romeo), and their friends were going to the party. Mercutio loved to talk. He enjoyed making funny speeches.

Romeo was in love, but he wasn't happy. Rosaline would never love any man. Mercutio told him not to take love so seriously.

Romeo did not have a good feeling about going to the Capulets'. Something bad might come of it.

ROMEO: Peace, peace, Mercutio, peace!
Thou talkest of nothing.
MERCUTIO: True. I talk of dreams;
Which are the children of an idle brain,
Begot of nothing but vain fantasy…

At the Capulets' party, Romeo took one look at Juliet and fell in love. He thought Juliet was the most beautiful girl he had ever seen.

Juliet was dancing. He watched her. As soon as he got the chance, he would go and stand near Juliet. All he wanted was to try to touch her hand.

ROMEO: The measure done, I'll watch her place of stand
And, touching hers, make blessed my rude hand.
Did my heart love till now? Forswear it, sight!
For I ne'er saw true beauty till this night.

Tybalt recognised Romeo! He wanted to throw him out. Romeo was a Montague. Tybalt wanted to start a fight. Old Capulet told him not to spoil the party. He said Tybalt should remember about good manners.

Tybalt kept talking about fighting Romeo. He wouldn't shut up. Old Capulet got very angry. He ordered Tybalt to leave.

Tybalt left, in a very bad mood. He would get Romeo later.

After the dance, Romeo stood near Juliet. He touched her hand. They talked.

Soon, they were kissing. Juliet wasn't thinking about the County Paris. Romeo forgot about Rosaline. Neither of them had ever felt like this before.

Too late, Romeo found out that Juliet was a Capulet.

Juliet found out that Romeo was a Montague.

Their families hated each other. They were falling in love. What could they do?

TYBALT: Patience perforce with wilful choler meeting
Makes my flesh tremble in their different greeting.
I will withdraw. But this intrusion shall,
Now seeming sweet, convert to bitterest gall.

ACT 2

After the party, Romeo hid from his friends and waited near Juliet's house. Juliet came out of her bedroom, on to the balcony. How beautiful she was. She was speaking aloud. She didn't know that Romeo was listening to her.

Juliet said that she loved Romeo. She was a Capulet. He was a Montague. Why should their names make any difference? They were still the same people. She loved him!

Romeo could not hide any longer. He was overjoyed. He cried out that if Juliet loved him, he would stop being a Montague.

Suddenly, Juliet was worried. If any of her family caught Romeo near her house, they would kill him.

They spoke of their love for each other. The nurse called. Juliet went inside, then came back again.

They didn't want to say goodnight. They were in love. They wanted to be married.

At last, they said goodnight and Juliet went to bed. Romeo went to see Friar Laurence. Perhaps Friar Laurence could help the lovers.

JULIET: Romeo, doff thy name;
         And for this name, which is no part of thee,
         Take all myself.
ROMEO: I take thee at thy word,
         Call me but love, and I'll be new baptized.
         Henceforth I never will be Romeo.

Friar Lawrence was in his garden. In those days, priests were like doctors. They looked after sick people. They made medicines from plants. The juices of plants could make people better, or they could make people sick. Friar Laurence knew all about these medicines.

FRIAR: Within the infant rind of this weak flower
Poison hath residence and medicine power.

Romeo told Friar Laurence that he was in love with Juliet. They wanted to be married. Friar Laurence was very surprised. Romeo had been in love with Rosaline. Could Romeo change his mind so quickly?

Friar Laurence was a good man. The fighting between the Capulets and the Montagues was wrong. If Romeo and Juliet were married, the Capulets and the Montagues might become friends. They couldn't go on hating each other. That is what Friar Laurence hoped.

He agreed to help Romeo and Juliet. He would marry them. Romeo was in a great hurry. Friar Laurence told him to slow down!

ROMEO: O, let us hence! I stand on sudden haste.
FRIAR: Wisely and slow. They stumble that run fast.

Romeo met Benvolio and Mercutio. They had no idea that he was in love with Juliet.

Juliet's nurse came along with her servant Peter. The young men teased her. Romeo knew that she was Juliet's messenger. He waited until Mercutio and Benvolio went away.

He gave the nurse two messages. First, Juliet was to go to Friar Laurence's that afternoon. Friar Laurence would marry them.

Second, he had a rope ladder. The nurse had to get the rope ladder from his servant. Romeo planned to climb the rope ladder to Juliet's bedroom. They would be together.

Romeo and Juliet – husband and wife.

ROMEO: Bid her devise
Some means to come to shrift this afternoon,
And there she shall at Friar Laurence' cell
Be shrived and married.

Juliet was waiting for the nurse to come back. She wanted to hear news of Romeo.

When she came back, the nurse chattered as usual. She was tired. She was out of breath. Romeo was wonderful. She had a headache. Where was Lady Capulet?

Juliet was frantic[1]. She wanted to know what Romeo had said.

At last, the nurse gave Juliet the two messages. First, Juliet was to tell her parents that she was going to see Friar Laurence. She was really going there to marry Romeo.

Second, the nurse was getting the rope ladder from Romeo's servant. Romeo and Juliet would be together that night.

[1]frantic – very excited and worried

NURSE: Jesu, what haste! Can you not stay a while?
Do you not see that I am out of breath?
JULIET: How art thou out of breath when thou hast breath
To say to me that thou art out of breath?
The excuse that thou dost make in this delay
Is longer than the tale thou dost excuse.
Is thy news good or bad? Answer to that.

Romeo and Juliet met at Friar Laurence's. He could see how much they loved each other. He took them to his chapel[1]. They would be married straight away.

[1]chapel – a small church

JULIET: They are but beggars that can count their worth.
But my true love is grown to such excess
I cannot sum up sum of half my wealth.
FRIAR: Come, come with me, and we will make short work.
For, by your leaves, you shall not stay alone
Till Holy Church incorporate two in one.

ACT 3

Mercutio, Benvolio and their Montague men met Tybalt and his Capulet men. Tybalt and Mercutio started to quarrel. Benvolio didn't want another fight. He tried to make them be sensible.

Romeo arrived. He had just married Juliet. He did not want to quarrel with Tybalt. Tybalt was Juliet's cousin.

Tybalt called Romeo a villain. Romeo refused to get into a fight with Tybalt.

Mercutio called Tybalt "King of Cats". They fought.

Romeo tried to stop the fight. He ran between them. Tybalt pushed his sword under Romeo's arm. He gave Mercutio a fatal[1] wound.

[1]fatal – causing death

ROMEO: Draw, Benvolio. Beat down their weapons.
Gentlemen, for shame! Forbear this outrage!
Tybalt, Mercutio, the Prince expressly hath
Forbid this bandying in Verona's streets.
Hold, Tybalt! Good Mercutio.

Mercutio was dying. He was very angry.

Why had Romeo got in the way? Tybalt stabbed Mercutio under Romeo's arm.

Mercutio cursed[1] the Capulets and the Montagues. He was dying because of their quarrel.

[1]curse – to wish bad things to happen

MERCUTIO: A plague a' both your houses! Zounds, a dog, a rat, a mouse, a cat to scratch a man to death! A braggart, a rogue, a villain, that fights by the book of arithmetic! Why the devil came you between us? I was hurt under your arm.

ROMEO: I thought all for the best.

Now, Romeo was angry too. He was angry with himself. Because he loved Juliet, Romeo had not fought Tybalt. He had been too soft. His dear friend, Mercutio, was dead.

Tybalt came back. This time, Romeo fought with him. Romeo killed Tybalt.

Benvolio reminded Romeo what the Prince had said about fighting. Death for those who started fights! Romeo had to get away.

BENVOLIO: Romeo, away, be gone!
The citizens are up, and Tybalt slain.
Stand not amazed. The Prince will doom thee death
If thou art taken. Hence, be gone, away!
ROMEO: O, I am fortune's fool!
BENVOLIO: Why dost thou stay?

The news soon spread. There had been more fighting. The Prince, Old Montague, Old Capulet, their wives and the people of Verona went to the town square.

Benvolio told the Prince what had happened: Tybalt started the fight. Romeo didn't want a fight. Tybalt and Mercutio fought. Romeo tried to stop them. Tybalt ran his sword under Romeo's arm and killed Mercutio. In revenge[1], Romeo killed Tybalt.

The Prince listened very carefully. He tried to be fair. Romeo had killed Tybalt in revenge for killing Mercutio. Therefore, the Prince said that Romeo would not die. Instead, he would be exiled[2] – he would have to leave Verona. If he was found in Verona, he would be killed.

[1]revenge – to get one's own back
[2]exiled – sent away from one's home place

PRINCE: Let Romeo hence in haste,
Else, when he is found, that hour is his last.
Bear hence this body, and attend our will.
Mercy but murders, pardoning those that kill.

Juliet was waiting for night to come. She was waiting for Romeo.

The nurse went to get the rope ladder. She returned with terrible news. Romeo had killed Tybalt. The Prince had sent Romeo away from Verona forever. He was banished[1].

Tybalt was Juliet's cousin. Romeo was her husband. Her husband had killed her cousin. She was very upset.

At first, she was angry with Romeo. Then she thought about it a bit more. She knew that Tybalt must have started the fight. She didn't blame Romeo.

Romeo had been sent away forever. Juliet said the word over and over, "Banished, banished, banished."

Juliet still wanted to be with Romeo that night. It would be their first and only time together.

[1]banished – sent away, exiled.

NURSE: Hie to your chamber. I'll find Romeo
To comfort you. I wot well where he is.
Hark ye, your Romeo will be here at night.
I'll to him. He is hid at Laurence' cell.
JULIET: O, find him! Give this ring to my true knight
And bid him come to take his last farewell.

Romeo went to see Friar Laurence. Friar Laurence told him about the Prince's punishment. Romeo was not to die, but he had to leave Verona forever. Romeo wanted to kill himself.

The nurse came with a message from Juliet.

Friar Laurence reminded Romeo that he had many things to be thankful for. Most important, he was still alive.

Romeo could spend the night with Juliet. He must remember to leave early. He must not be seen.

Friar Laurence had a plan. Romeo was to go to a town called Mantua. The Friar would send him news. There would soon be a chance to tell everyone about the marriage. The Prince would let Romeo come back. The Friar was sure everything would be all right!

Romeo felt happier. The nurse gave him the ring from Juliet. They would be together that night.

The Friar told him again to leave early in the morning.

FRIAR: Go, get thee to thy love, as was decreed.
Ascend her chamber. Hence and comfort her.
But look thou stay not till the Watch be set,
For then thou canst not pass to Mantua,
Where thou shalt live till we can find a time
To blaze your marriage, reconcile your friends,
Beg pardon of the Prince, and call thee back
With twenty hundred thousand times more joy
Than thou wentest forth in lamentation.

The Capulets had a visitor – the County Paris. It was now early the next morning.

Paris asked again to marry Juliet. This time, Lord Capulet agreed. The wedding would be three days later.

Before Lady Capulet went to bed, she was to go and tell Juliet. The Capulets thought that Juliet would be happy.

They didn't know that Juliet was already married to Romeo.

They didn't know that Romeo and Juliet were together at that very moment. Romeo was supposed to leave very early in the morning. Would he leave in time?

CAPULET: Well, get you gone. A'Thursday be it, then.
Go you to Juliet ere you go to bed.
Prepare her , wife, against this wedding day.
Farewell, my lord. – Light to my chamber, ho!
Afore me, it is so very late that we
May call it early by and by. Good night.

It was almost daylight. Romeo and Juliet were saying goodbye. They could not bear to part. Romeo must go away to Mantua. When would they see each other again?

The nurse came to tell them that Lady Capulet was coming to see Juliet.

Quickly, Romeo left. He didn't know that the Capulets were planning Juliet's marriage to Paris.

JULIET: Wilt thou be gone? It is not yet near day.
It was the nightingale and not the lark,
That pierced the fearful hollow of thine ear.
Nightly she sings on yond pomegranate tree.
Believe me, love, it was the nightingale.

Lady Capulet came to see Juliet. Romeo had just left.

Juliet was crying. She pretended that she was crying about Tybalt. She was really crying for Romeo.

Lady Capulet told Juliet that she was to marry Paris in three days' time. Juliet was taken by surprise. She said that she could never marry Paris.

Juliet had a terrible row with her father. On her knees, she asked him not to make her marry Paris. Her father became furious. He shouted at her. He would throw her out on to the streets. She could starve and die.

Juliet tried to talk to her mother. Lady Capulet sided with her husband.

Juliet had always tried to please her parents. Now, they were angry and disappointed. What had happened to Juliet?

Her parents left, and Juliet talked to the nurse. The nurse said that Juliet should marry Paris. This was very bad advice. Juliet was already married to Romeo. To marry again was against the laws of the Church.

Juliet went to see Friar Laurence. If there was no other way, she would kill herself. She could not marry Paris. She was married to Romeo.

JULIET: Good father, I beseech you on my knees,
Hear me with patience but to speak a word.

ACT 4

Friar Laurence had heard about the wedding. He had another plan. He knew a lot about plants and medicines. He had a special sleeping potion[1] to make Juliet look as if she was dead. She would not be dead. After forty-two hours, she would wake up.

Friar Laurence told Juliet to drink the potion the night before her wedding. Everyone would think she was dead. Instead of a wedding, there would have to be a funeral. Juliet's "body" would be put in the Capulets' family vault[2].

Friar Laurence planned to send a messenger to Romeo. Romeo would come back to Verona to be with Juliet when she woke up. They could go away together.

Juliet was very brave. She agreed to the plan.

[1]sleeping potion – a special drink to make you sleep.
[2]vault – a kind of underground room where rich families put
      their dead people.

FRIAR: Now, when the bridegroom in the morning comes
To rouse thee from thy bed, thou art dead.
Then, as the manner of our country is,
In thy best robes uncovered on the bier
Thou shalt be borne to that same ancient vault
Where all the kindred of the Capulets lie.

Juliet told her father she was sorry. She would do as he wished. He was very happy. The wedding would be the very next day.

That night, Juliet got ready to take the Friar's potion. Would it work? What if she really died? Or woke up in the family vault with dead bodies around her. What if she died from lack of air before Romeo came? She might go mad. Juliet was very frightened.

She thought about her Romeo. She drank the potion.

JULIET: Romeo, Romeo, Romeo.
Here's drink. I drink to thee.

Next morning, the Capulets were getting ready for Juliet's wedding. They were very happy.

The nurse, chattering as usual, went to get Juliet out of bed. Juliet didn't wake up. The nurse thought she was dead.

The nurse screamed and cried. The Capulets came rushing in. Friar Laurence and County Paris arrived. Everyone was crying. They were sure Juliet was dead.

All the happy things planned for the day turned to sad things. The music, the flowers, the singing were all now for a funeral instead of a wedding. Everything was opposite.

Instead of being married, Juliet would be put in the family vault. Only Friar Laurence knew that she was not really dead.

CAPULET: All things that we ordained festival
           Turn from their office to black funeral.
           Our instruments to melancholy bells;
           Our wedding cheer to a sad burial feast;
           Our solemn hymns to sullen dirges change;
           Our bridal flowers serve for a buried corse;
           And all things change them to the contrary.

ACT 5

Romeo's servant, Balthasar, saw Juliet's funeral. He saw Juliet's body put in the family vault. He thought Juliet was really dead. He didn't know about the Friar's plan. He rode to tell Romeo straight away.

Balthasar told Romeo all the bad news. He told Romeo that his wife Juliet was dead. Twice, Romeo asked if he had letters from the Friar. Balthasar knew only what he had seen. He had no messages from the Friar.

Romeo sent Balthasar to get horses. Romeo wanted to go and see Juliet's body in the family vault.

He went to find an apothecary[1].

[1]apothecary – someone who knows about drugs and medicines; a chemist.

BALTHASAR: Her body sleeps in Capel's monument,
And her immortal parts with angels lives.
I saw her laid low in her kindred's vault
And presently took post to tell it you.

Romeo went to the apothecary and bought a very strong poison. Selling poison was against the law. Romeo paid the apothecary a lot of money.

This was not like the potion Juliet had taken. This was real poison.

Romeo planned to go to the Capulet family vault, take the poison and die beside his wife, Juliet.

APOTHECARY: Put this in any liquid thing you will
And drink it off, and if you had the strength
Of twenty men it would dispatch you straight.

Friar Laurence had sent a letter to Romeo, telling him that Juliet wasn't really dead. He gave the letter to a man named Friar John.

Friar John didn't get to Mantua. He gave the letter back to Friar Laurence.

Friar Laurence was very worried. Romeo had not received his message. Romeo thought that Juliet was dead. What would he do?

Friar Laurence hurried to the vault to be there when Juliet woke up.

FRIAR LAURENCE: Unhappy fortune! By my brotherhood,
The letter was not nice, but full of charge,
Of dear import; and the neglecting it
May do much danger. Friar John, go
hence.
Get me an iron crow and bring it straight
Unto my cell.

Romeo & Juliet

Romeo went to the vault. He planned to take the poison and die beside Juliet.

Paris was also at the vault. He tried to stop Romeo going in. They fought and Romeo killed Paris. As he lay dying, Paris asked Romeo to put his body in the vault.

Romeo went down into the vault. He dragged Paris's body in as well.

He looked at Juliet. She was so beautiful lying there. She didn't look dead. He wanted to stay with her. He didn't know she was only sleeping and would soon wake up.

He kissed her goodbye and took the poison. He died immediately.

Just too late, Friar Laurence came along. He saw Romeo and Paris, both dead.

At that moment, Juliet woke up.

Night watchmen were coming. Friar Laurence wanted Juliet to leave with him. No one knew she was alive. He could help her to get away. She could go to a convent[1].

Seeing Romeo dead, Juliet refused to leave.

Juliet heard a night watchman coming. There was no poison left. She took Romeo's dagger and killed herself.

[1]convent – a place where women live together to worship God.

ROMEO: Here's to my love! O true Apothecary!
Thy drugs are quick. Thus with a kiss I die.

The people of Verona went to the Capulets' tomb. Old Capulet, Lady Capulet, the Prince and Old Montague were all there. Lady Montague was dead. She died of grief[1] because Romeo was sent away.

The Friar was the only one who knew the whole story. He told the Prince and the two families about all the things that had happened. Romeo and Juliet had loved each other and he had tried to be helpful. He married them. All they wanted was to be together. Everything had gone wrong and now they were dead.

The Prince told the Montagues and the Capulets that this sad ending was because of their fighting. He, too, should have been stronger in stopping the fighting. Now, they have all been punished.

The death of Romeo and Juliet brought everyone to their senses. No one wanted to fight anymore.

Old Capulet said he would put up a beautiful gold statue of Romeo. Old Montague said that he would put up a beautiful gold statue of Juliet.

But nothing could bring them back to life. Romeo and Juliet were dead.

---

[1]grief – sadness

PRINCE: Capulet, Montague,
See what a scourge is laid upon your hate,
That heaven finds means to kill your joys with love.
And I, for winking at your discords too,
Have lost a brace of kinsmen. All are punished.

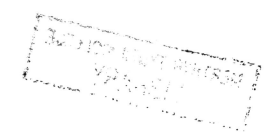